This Little Tiger book belongs to:

_____

_____

_____

To my dad, thanks for everything! – S S

For my dad, Phillip 'Juggy' Julian – S J

LITTLE TIGER PRESS
1 The Coda Centre, 189 Munster Road, London SW6 6AW
www.littletiger.co.uk
First published in Great Britain 2012
This edition published 2016
Text copyright © Steve Smallman 2012 • Illustrations copyright © Sean Julian 2012
Steve Smallman and Sean Julian have asserted their rights to be
identified as the author and illustrator of this work under
the Copyright, Designs and Patents Act, 1988

My Dad!

Steve Smallman   Sean Julian

LITTLE TIGER PRESS
London

Some dads will give you
enormous great
cuddles.

Some dads join in when you're jumping in puddles.

Some dads will run up
and down by your side,
Holding your bike till you
learn how to ride.

Some dads can cheer you up
when you are crying,

And hold you **so high**
that you feel like you're flying!

Some dads will help you
whatever you do.

tRUMP!

Some dads will trump
and then say it was you!

Some dads build magical castles of sand,

Or make you feel safe
just by holding
your hand.

Some dads drink soda
and give you a slurp,
And then laugh out loud
when you do a big burp!

Some dads look **BIG** as a GIANT to you, And up on their shoulders you feel like one too!

Some dads get cross
and start sulking
and stamping,

GRRRRRRRRR!

Just because they're a
bit rubbish at camping!

Some dads try hard
but they really
can't cook,

And some dads are
brilliant at reading a book.

Nobody's dad is like mine and I'm glad.

When I'm big I want to be **just** *like* *my* dad!